CHAPTER 1

"Lisa! Lisa, I'm not going to call you again. You'll be late on your first day back at school. Do you want me to come up there?" called Lisa's mother from the foot of the stairs.

"I'm up, okay", replied Lisa as she rolled out of her warm, cosy bed and walked across the hall onto the cold bathroom tiles.

After she had washed and dressed into her school uniform, she looked at her reflection in the bedroom mirror. "I'm so glad that I'll be able to wear trousers next year, instead of these short skirts", she thought.

The school had changed its rules that year to allow trousers too. But Lisa's mother had said that because her skirt was almost new, she must wait another year before she could wear trousers to school.

Lisa sauntered along to the kitchen and sat down at the table.

"Has Dad gone then?" she asked.

THE MEAT EATING VEGETARIAN

by
Caroline Maryam Ward

THE MEAT EATING VEGETARIAN
By: Caroline Maryam Ward
Illustrations: Asiya Clarke 2001

A CIP record for this title is available from the British Library

ISBN 0-86037-306-1

Published by
The Islamic Foundation, Markfield Conference Centre
Ratby Lane, Markfield, Leicestershire LE67 9SY, United Kingdom
Tel: (01530) 244944 Fax: (01530) 244946
E-mail: i.foundation@islamic-foundation.org.uk
Website: www.islamic-foundation.org.uk

Quran House, PO Box 30611, Nairobi, Kenya

PMB 3193, Kano, Nigeria

"I should think so. Do you know what time it is? You've only got 25 minutes to eat that and run to school. You should have had a good breakfast on your first day back at least", said Lisa's mother as she pushed a plate of toast over to her.

Lisa started to nibble a slice of toast, but she felt too anxious to eat. She had that fluttery feeling in her stomach and could think only of the new class she would be in, if her friend Yvonne would be able to sit next to her, and how she would feel if Yvonne was not in her class at all that year.

"Mum, do you think Yvonne will be in my class?" asked Lisa anxiously.

"I don't know. Look Lisa, it's quarter to

nine and I have to go. I'll pick up some chops for dinner. We can have a nice meal tonight and you can tell me all about how you got on at school today, okay? You'll be fine, you'll see. Don't forget to put the double lock on the door when you go, sweetheart. I'll see you tonight." Lisa's mother kissed her cheek as she grabbed her handbag and struggled into her coat.

Oh well, at least there was a nice family dinner to look forward to! Crispy gristly-edged chops, all soft and juicy in the middle, served with buttery mashed potatoes, broccoli and salad was something to take her mind off her worries, and Lisa finally rushed into school just as the bell was ringing.

CHAPTER 2

Miss Parkin was the new teacher for
Lisa's class. Her seating plan was
alphabetical as she said this was fair for
everyone. Fair? thought Lisa as she took
a seat at the back of the class and
watched Yvonne take hers on the
second row from the front. She could
not even pass a note to Yvonne, and

had to be happy with waving to her instead. At least they were in the same class.

"Hi!" said the girl sitting in the seat next to Lisa.

"Hi", replied Lisa as she turned to look at her. The girl sitting next to her was new and she had a headscarf on. Before she could stop herself she found herself blurting out, "Where are you from?"

"England", came the reply.

"Oh. Err, I mean like where did you come from before you came to England?"

"I was born here, and my family is from Pakistan."

"Yeah, that's what I meant. Is that why they make you wear a scarf?"

"No. I wear it because I'm a Muslim. It has nothing to do with where I come from."

"Oh, right. So what's your name?"

"Tasneem", replied the girl.

"Well, I'm Lisa, and I did *not* want to be sitting here. My best mate is up there in the second row", Lisa blurted out and then regretted what she had said when she saw the hurt look on Tasneem's face.

"Oh sorry, I didn't mean … You know, about you or anything. It's just…"
Unable to find the words for what she meant, Lisa let the last sentence trail off feebly.

"It's okay really, I know what you meant. We've only just moved into the area and I don't know anyone here at all. I was so worried about coming to such a big school, but now that I've met you it doesn't seem so bad any more", said Tasneem enthusiastically.

Lisa smiled. It would be good to be friends with someone like Tasneem, who didn't want to jump on everything you said and make something out of it. She liked this new girl already. Perhaps things would work out after all.

During the morning Miss Parkin made everyone write essays about what they had done in the summer holidays. Lisa had not been away as such, but her parents had taken her to the park for fun and picnics whenever they were not working. They had even gone fishing once and Lisa had caught a fish on a real fishing line. Yvonne had been to Jamaica to visit her grandparents so she had a lot to write about. Tasneem had been busy with the move from a town four hours drive away, so the summer had been one long time of living in and out of boxes and not being able to find things, until she had finally settled in her new home.

Everyone was so busy writing they hardly noticed the time fly by as they relived the excitement and sometimes disappointments that had gone on during the last six weeks. They had been told to do an illustration too, one that pictured the most important part of their story. Lisa had drawn the fishing rod and the fish she had caught.

Yvonne did a beach with a palm tree and tropical sunset, and Tasneem drew a box which had a label on it saying CLOTHES, but showed its contents to be plates and cups instead!

CHAPTER 3

The lunch bell sounded and the class was dismissed by the teacher. Everyone put their stationary away and rushed towards the door. Tasneem followed the others unsure of where to go. Lisa ran over to Yvonne in the corridor and the two began chattering excitedly. When they reached the canteen door Tasneem was behind them. Lisa caught her eye.

"Oh yeah Yvonne, this is Tasneem. She's sitting next to me."

"You can come on our table for lunch if you like", Lisa said to Tasneem.

"Thanks, I'd like that", replied Tasneem and she smiled at them both.

"Hi, I'm Yvonne", said the other girl as she smiled back warmly.

They filed into the canteen, collected trays and cutlery and stood in line waiting their turn in the serving queue. Tasneem reached the counter first.

"Meat pie or sausages?" asked the dinner lady kindly.

"No thank you. Vegetarian please", replied Tasneem.

"Just mash and salad then. There we are. Move along there now, love. Next."

Tasneem moved to the side to wait for Lisa and Yvonne who were busy making sense of what they had just heard.

"What's a vegetarian?" Lisa asked Yvonne.

"Someone who doesn't eat meat", replied Yvonne. "Go on, let's ask her about it."

"Oh, no! I've put my foot in it so much with Tasneem already, but she was okay about it. Anyway, all this about the headscarf and stuff is fine but if you

can't eat meat that's something I really
don't want to be included in", said Lisa
as her thoughts wondered back to her
mother's promise of the nice family
dinner that evening.

"Shush Lisa, she'll hear us. Come on,
let's sit down. She's waiting", said
Yvonne.

The three girls took their places at a
table near the window. They chatted
and giggled together while they ate, and
by the end of the meal were all good
friends.

CHAPTER 4

The first week of school was nearly over
and the three girls met up every
playtime and lunch to laugh, talk and
play. It seemed as if they had known
each other for ages and had formed a
strong and easy bond of friendship.

On Friday morning Tasneem came

charging into the playground and nearly bowled the others over. She was almost bursting with some kind of news!

"Guess what? My Mum said you could all come round on Monday night for dinner. We could eat and then play in my room, and I could show you all the stuff I was telling you about. We can even play with the board games now they're all unpacked. Oh please, please say you will!" gushed Tasneem.

"Yeah, of course!" said Lisa happily.

"Great! I'm sure my Mum will let me", replied Yvonne.

"Oh, I'll have to ask as well, but Monday isn't anything special at our house, so she'll probably let me", said Lisa.

"Fantastic. Oh, I just can't wait",
Tasneem sighed.

During that playtime and lunch the girls
talked about how to get to Tasneem's
house and what they would do together
for the visit.

The weekend dragged by for a change,
and on Monday after school the final
arrangements were made.

"Yvonne's coming round to mine Tas,
and then my Dad's going to drop us off at
yours at five o'clock, okay? He's going
bowling so he won't have to pick us up
'till after half past eight!" said Lisa
excitedly.

"Brilliant! Okay then, see you all later",
said Tasneem as she rushed home.

Tasneem's mother had been busy all day, preparing for the meal. Hospitality is a big issue in Muslim homes and Tasneem's mother loved entertaining and pleasing her guests. Today was especially important as her daughter had made new friends and she was determined to make them feel welcome and happy.

At 5.15pm the doorbell rang and the girls piled into Tasneem's hall.

CHAPTER 5

Lisa was surprised to see Tasneem
without her scarf on. She said nothing,
but saw that Yvonne had noticed it too.

"Hey you two, here at last! Come on
into the dining room. I'm starving", said
Tasneem.

The two slightly nervous guests followed Tasneem through to the dining room. Lisa was wondering what vegetarians would serve as a whole meal. She felt worried in case she was asked to eat plates of vegetables on their own.Yvonne's mind was running along similar lines and imagining great piles of grated carrots and chopped lettuce!

Just then Tasneem's mother pushed through the swing doors of the kitchen carrying a large platter of lamb burgers.

"I've made Tasneem's favourite. I hope you like lamb burgers girls, you've plenty to get through!"

She was followed by Tasneem with an even larger platter of chips and a bowl of a very exotic looking salad which she placed in the middle of the table.

"Oops. I forgot the relish. Hang on a minute ... or start eating if you don't need any relish", said Tasneem as she disappeared back through the doors which swung shut behind her.

Lisa and Yvonne exchanged looks.

"She's not a vegetarian at all. What a liar!" whispered Lisa. "And her scarf, if she has to wear it all the time, where is it? She never takes it off at school. She's just a fake!"

"She was pretending at school all along", replied Yvonne, "to make herself more important than us".

"We'll go home right after dinner, okay. I'm not staying round here if she thinks she can fool us like that!" said Lisa.

Tasneem came back with the relish and loaded her plate with a lamb burger and lots of chips and salad. She was always so hungry when she came home from school and today's meal was later than usual. She did not notice her friends' change of feeling towards her.

Throughout the meal Lisa and Yvonne exchanged looks as Tasneem talked about her Mum's cooking, and how she was famous for her Chicken Curry and special fried meat balls that they usually had on Fridays. By the end of the meal Lisa was seething with pent up anger and Yvonne was trying to think of an excuse to leave.

In the end it was Lisa who walked to the door and started to put on her coat.

"We have to go now. I don't feel well. Can your Mum drop us back because my Dad won't be back from bowling yet?"

"But we haven't done anything yet. Lisa what's wrong? Sit down you'll feel better after dinner has settled down a bit," said Tasneem.

"Um, she wasn't feeling well earlier actually. I think your Mum had better drop us back home. Please Tasneem we just want to go", said Yvonne.

Reluctantly Tasneem went to her mother to explain. Mrs. Abdullah came rushing into the hall. But despite many offers of comfort and treatment the girls were almost pleading now to be taken home.

"We can arrange another visit, Tasneem. It is more important that Lisa is taken care of where she wants to be. At home", said Tasneem's mother.

Lisa was feeling quite guilty herself now. Mrs. Abdullah seemed to be really nice. How could Tasneem be so different? She was angry, confused and upset.

Lisa and Yvonne got into the car. Tasneem's mother rushed upstairs and took a small blanket and pillow and tucked Lisa up in the back seat before driving off. Lisa felt even more guilty now, and could not meet Tasneem's eyes, so she decided not to wave or look back as the car pulled away from the house.

Tasneem was left on the doorstep
looking at the red taillights of the car as
they disappeared into the distance. The
wonderful evening she had so carefully
planned seemed to fade away with the
lights of the car.

CHAPTER 6

The next day Tasneem ran up to her two friends in the playground.

"Glad you came today Lisa, I thought you might still be in bed. How are you feeling?"

"Fine", replied Lisa coldly.

"When can you come again?" asked Tasneem.

"We can't", said Yvonne.

Lisa was now even more angry than before as she had thought about all the times Tasneem had lied to her about the scarf and about the food. She felt cheated and tricked. Now that Mrs. Abdullah was not there smoothing everything away and being kind and nice, Lisa felt furious.

"You tell her Yvonne. I don't talk to liars", said Lisa.

"We don't want to be friends with you any more. You make up stories so that everyone thinks you're special. You're such a liar, and a bad one at that. Didn't you think we would find you out? Do you think we're stupid?" said Yvonne angrily.

Tasneem reeled back from their words. Tears sprung to her eyes.

"No, I don't think that. I thought you liked me. I'm not a liar, how can you say that I am?" Tasneem's voice was shaking.

Lisa and Yvonne turned and walked away. Tasneem looked at them in hurt and confusion, her head bent down, she was unable to stop the tears from running down her cheeks.

All that morning Tasneem tried smiling at her former friends but her attempts were met with cold looks. In the queue at lunchtime, she could hear what they were saying. When Tasneem's turn came to be served, she passed her plate over to the dinner lady.

"Chicken or meat balls, love?" asked the dinner lady.

"No thank you. Vegetarian please", replied Tasneem.

"Oh. Pasta's over there, love, and the cheese sauce is at the end of the counter. Next."

"She's still doing it", fumed Lisa.

"What a fake!" said Yvonne.

When Tasneem heard this she was even

more confused. What had she done? How could ordering her lunch make them sound so angry?

Sitting at the same table was almost unbearable. Tasneem tried to eat and kept her head down to avoid their eyes. As soon as she could, she took her tray back and ran out into the playground, then across it and into the cloakroom. She sat down and sobbed. This felt unreal, like she was watching it happen to someone else. It had come like a bolt of lightening out of nowhere. How? What had she done?

CHAPTER 7

"Tasneem! What are you doing in here?
You know the cloakroom is out of
bounds during playtime", said Miss
Parkin as she came in and saw her
sitting in a corner.

Tasneem lifted her head. Tears were

streaming down her red and swollen face.

"Sorry, Miss", she sobbed.

"Oh Tasneem! Whatever is the matter?" asked Miss Parkin as her annoyance turned to concern when she saw the pitiful state her pupil was in.

"Nothing", said Tasneem woodenly.

"Well, that's a lot of tears over nothing. Come on with me. I've got to go back to the classroom. We'll talk about it there. I've a box of tissues in my desk and you look like you need a few", said Miss Parkin kindly.

Back in the classroom, Miss Parkin sat

Tasneem down and gave her some tissues.

"Come on now, are you going to tell me what's happened?" asked Miss Parkin gently.

Tasneem blew her nose and wiped her face with the tissues.

"They liked me before. We had a lovely time and I really like them. Then they said I'm a liar and tell stories and make things up, and that I want to be special", blurted out Tasneem with a big sob, and fresh tears sprung to her eyes.

"Can you tell me who said those things to you? Is someone bullying you Tasneem?"

Tasneem tried hard to pull herself together. She felt silly and babyish crying like this in front of Miss Parkin.

"No. It's not like that. I don't think they are. Lisa and Yvonne were my best friends. We did everything together. Then after they came to my house for dinner they didn't like me any more and said all those horrible things to me. Today in the lunch queue I could hear them talking about me. All I did was order my lunch, and they said I'm still doing it and what a faker I am, and I didn't even say anything to them."

"What did you say to the dinner lady?" asked Miss Parkin.

"I just asked for my lunch. Vegetarian, like always", replied Tasneem.

"I see, and what did you have for dinner when the girls came to your house?"

"Lamb burgers, chips and stuff like that. My mother cooked the burgers herself because the ones in the supermarket are not halal for us you know, so she gets the mince from the *halal* butcher and spices it herself. It was such a lovely meal. We were going to do loads of things together after, but as soon as dinner was finished Lisa felt sick and she wanted to go home, so they both left. Then today they've been so horrible to me and I don't know why."

"I think I know what's happened Tasneem", said Miss Parkin. "Look, I want you to go and wash your face, okay? Then come straight back here. I think we can sort this out. Run along now, off you go!"

CHAPTER 8

Tasneem did as she was told and when she came back to the classroom, Lisa and Yvonne were both there. Miss Parkin smiled and told Tasneem to come in.

"Now girls. I have called you all here because I think there has been a big misunderstanding between you. Lisa and Yvonne, you have made Tasneem very upset by your behaviour", said Miss Parkin.

At this, Lisa could no longer contain herself. She stood up and turned angrily on Tasneem.

"She's the one who's causing the trouble Miss, not us!" burst out Lisa. "Whatever she said about us, it's a lie! We didn't do anything wrong. You can't believe her, she's such a liar. You can't trust anything she says!"

"That's enough Lisa. This is exactly what I've been talking about. You are jumping to conclusions before you've even finished listening to what I have to say", replied Miss Parkin.

Lisa sat down and glared at Tasneem. Yvonne looked down nervously.

"Now, as I was saying, there has been a misunderstanding. Both of you liked Tasneem well enough before you went to her house for dinner. Then something you saw there changed your mind, and then today in the lunch queue you thought your suspicions were right. Is that what happened?"

Lisa and Yvonne were speechless. Miss Parkin sounded like a mind reader!

When there was no reply from either of them and Miss Parkin continued.

"Tasneem. Are you a vegetarian?"

"No", said Tasneem. "I do eat meat but

it has to be *halal.* That means that you have to be kind to the animal, and before you kill it you have to say God's name. So, I can't eat any school meat because it's not halal."

"Well, Lisa ... Yvonne ... do you have anything else to say?"

"Yeah, okay. But what about your scarf then? You said you have to wear it all the time, but in your house you never had it on at all."

"I do like to wear it all the time when I'm outdoors, because my mum does, and I love her and want to be just like her. Really, Mum did say that I'm little and it doesn't matter because this rule is only for ladies and not girls", explained Tasneem. "You see, Muslim ladies wear their scarves outside their home, or when men they are not related to are around."

"Thank you, Tasneem", said Miss Parkin, and then she turned to Lisa and Yvonne, "Do you have any other matters to be cleared up? Do you both agree at least that there has been a misunderstanding between you and Tasneem?"

Lisa looked at Tasneem. She felt very sorry to see her swollen face and red eyes, and to think that she had been the cause of it.

"I am so sorry, Tasneem. I didn't know. I should have asked you first. I liked it when we were all friends, it was great! Then I felt cheated and used and angry.

I thought you had picked us to cheat on and make fools of", said Lisa, lowering her head and speaking almost to the floor instead of Tasneem.

"Yeah. We really got you wrong, Tasneem. I just thought you were pretending and trying to make us believe things that weren't true", said Yvonne.

"I'm sorry you didn't understand", said Tasneem. "I should have explained more, but I thought if I was always going on about myself and my religion and that, you'd get bored with me or something, so I try not to mention it too much."

"Yeah. You're right there, Tasneem. I know how that feels. My grandma back in Jamaica is really into her church and whenever we get to see her, we never hear about anything else", replied Yvonne with a smile.

"Well, that is better, I must say. I think this is an excellent opportunity for a little project. We have to do world religions in the National Curriculum and I think the one we will start with is Islam", said Miss Parkin happily, who never missed any gap where she could slip in something educational!

The bell rang just then, and the three girls went to their desks, firm in their friendship and in their understanding of each other.